Dear Parents and Educators,

Welcome to Penguin Young Readers! As parents and educators, you know that each child develops at his or her own pace—in terms of speech, critical thinking, and, of course, reading. Penguin Young Readers recognizes this fact. As a result, each Penguin Young Readers book is assigned a traditional easy-to-read level (1–4) as well as a Guided Reading Level (A–P). Both of these systems will help you choose the right book for your child. Please refer to the back of each book for specific leveling information. Penguin Young Readers features esteemed authors and illustrators, stories about favorite characters, fascinating nonfiction, and more!

Cork & Fuzz: Short and Tall

This book is perfect for a **Transitional Reader** who:

- can read multisyllable and compound words;
- can read words with prefixes and suffixes;
- is able to identify story elements (beginning, middle, end, plot, setting, characters, problem, solution); and
- can understand different points of view.

Here are some **activities** you can do during and after reading this book:

- Character Venn Diagrams: Cork and Fuzz are best friends. But there are lots of things about them that are different. On a separate sheet of paper, draw two overlapping circles. On top of one circle, write *Cork*. On top of the other circle, write *Fuzz*. In the space that overlaps, list the character traits that Cork and Fuzz share. In the spaces that don't overlap, list the character traits that are unique.
- Make Connections: Think about your best friend. How are you the same? How are you different? Discuss why you are friends.

Remember, sharing the love of reading with a child is the best gift you can give!

—Bonnie Bader, EdM
Penguin Young Readers program

*Penguin Young Readers are leveled by independent reviewers applying the standards developed by Irene Fountas and Gay Su Pinnell in *Matching Books to Readers: Using Leveled Books in Guided Reading*, Heinemann, 1999.

For Steven James, my star—DC

To Max, who'll be learning to read soon—LM

Penguin Young Readers
Published by the Penguin Group
Penguin Group (USA) Inc., 375 Hudson Street, New York, New York 10014, USA
Penguin Group (Canada), 90 Eglinton Avenue East, Suite 700, Toronto, Ontario M4P 2Y3, Canada
(a division of Pearson Penguin Canada Inc.)
Penguin Books Ltd, 80 Strand, London WC2R 0RL, England
Penguin Ireland, 25 St Stephen's Green, Dublin 2, Ireland (a division of Penguin Books Ltd)
Penguin Group (Australia), 707 Collins Street, Melbourne, Victoria 3008, Australia
(a division of Pearson Australia Group Pty Ltd)
Penguin Books India Pvt Ltd, 11 Community Centre, Panchsheel Park, New Delhi—110 017, India
Penguin Group (NZ), 67 Apollo Drive, Rosedale, Auckland 0632, New Zealand
(a division of Pearson New Zealand Ltd)
Penguin Books (South Africa), Rosebank Office Park, 181 Jan Smuts Avenue,
Parktown North 2193, South Africa
Penguin China, B7 Jiaming Center, 27 East Third Ring Road North,
Chaoyang District, Beijing 100020, China

Penguin Books Ltd, Registered Offices: 80 Strand, London WC2R 0RL, England

 First published in 2006 by Viking and in 2010 by Puffin Books, imprints of Penguin Group (USA) Inc. Published in 2013 by Penguin Young Readers, an imprint of Penguin Group (USA) Inc., 345 Hudson Street, New York, New York 10014. Manufactured in China.

The Library of Congress has cataloged the Viking edition
under the following Control Number: 2004017393

ISBN 978-0-14-241594-8 10 9 8 7 6 5 4 3 2 1

PENGUIN YOUNG READERS

LEVEL 3

TRANSITIONAL READER

CORK & FUZZ

Short and Tall

by Dori Chaconas

illustrated by Lisa McCue

Penguin Young Readers

An Imprint of Penguin Group (USA) Inc.

Chapter 1

Cork was a short muskrat.

He ate cattails and roots.

Fuzz was a tall possum.

He ate berries and seeds,

pancakes,

hamburger buns,

apple peels,

candy wrappers,

worms,

and black beetles.

One short muskrat.

One tall possum.

Two best friends.

One day, Cork looked up
at Fuzz's head.
"Something is not right," Cork said.
"What is not right?" Fuzz asked.
"I am older than you," Cork said.
"But you are taller than me."
"Are you standing in a hole?"
Fuzz asked.
Cork looked down.
"I am not standing in a hole.
You are taller than me."
"Does it matter that I am taller
than you?" Fuzz asked.
"I am older," Cork said.

"I need to be taller.

It is a rule."

"I am sorry," Fuzz said.

"I did not mean to break a rule."

"Do you think you can be shorter?"
Cork asked.
Fuzz's tail dropped into the dirt.
"I do not know how to be shorter,"
he said.
"Think, think, think," Cork said.
"We will think about how to make
you shorter."

"Lunch, lunch, lunch," Fuzz said.
"I will think about eating lunch."
He picked up a beetle.
He opened his mouth wide.
"Do not eat that beetle!"
Cork yelled.

He grabbed Fuzz's snout.

"If you stop eating, you will stop growing!

Then you will not be taller than me."

"Umma-umma-umma!"

Fuzz tried to speak.

Cork let go of Fuzz's snout.

"Stop eating?" Fuzz shouted. "Me?"

"Just for a little while," Cork said.

"How long is a little while?"

Fuzz looked worried.

"Not long," Cork said.

"About . . . seven days."

Fuzz groaned.

Chapter 2

"While we are waiting for you to not grow," Cork said, "can you walk on your knees?
That will make you shorter."
Fuzz groaned again.
Cork walked along the path on his feet.
Fuzz walked along the path on his knees.
"Ouch!" Fuzz said.
"What is the matter?" Cork asked.
"My knee stepped on a stick,"
Fuzz said.
They took three more steps.

Fuzz yelled again, “Ouch! Ouch!”

“What is the matter now?”

Cork asked.

“My knee stepped on a nut.”

They took three more steps.

Fuzz yelled again.

“Ouch! Ouch! *Ouch!*”

“What did your knee step on now?”

Cork asked.

“This time it is not my knee that

hurts,” Fuzz said.

“This time it is my stomach

that hurts, because it is empty!”

Cork sighed.

“This is not going to work.”

“I cannot be shorter,” Fuzz said.

“But maybe we can make you taller.”

“Oh yes,” said Cork.

“We can make me taller!”

“Possums eat good food!” Fuzz said.

“Maybe you need to eat

like a possum.

Then you will grow like a possum.”

"What did you eat for breakfast?"
Cork asked.
"I ate three beetles.
I ate four worms.
I ate two pancakes."
"I hope there are some
pancakes left," Cork said.
"Nope," said Fuzz.
"But here is a nice fat worm!"
"Uck," said Cork.
"Do I have to eat it?"
"Do you want to grow?" Fuzz asked.
"Yes," said Cork.
He closed his eyes.
He opened his mouth.

Chapter 3

"I cannot eat this worm!" Cork said.
"Maybe possums do something else
to make them tall."
Fuzz popped the worm
into his own mouth.
"We hang from tree branches,"
he said.
Cork jumped up and down.
"I can hang from a branch!" he said.
"I can stretch!"

"We hang by our tails," Fuzz said.

Cork looked at his short tail.

"My tail cannot do that."

"You can hang by your paws!"

Fuzz said.

Cork jumped up and down again.

"Yes!" he said.

"I can hang by my paws!"

Cork stood on Fuzz's back.

He grabbed a branch on the nut tree.

Fuzz moved away.

Cork's feet swung in the air.

"Do I have to hang here long?"

Cork asked.

"Not long," Fuzz said.

"About . . . seven days."

Cork wiggled.

“I have a problem.”

“What kind of problem?” Fuzz asked.

“A seed puff blew up my nose,”

Cork said.

“Now I have an itch.”

“Scratch it,” said Fuzz.

“If I scratch it, I will fall,” Cork said.

“Can you wait?” Fuzz asked.

"No," Cork said. "I cannot wait.

It is a bad itch."

"Can you sneeze it out?" Fuzz asked.

"Ka-*chee*!" Cork sneezed.

"Ka-*chee*!"

"I cannot sneeze it out!"

"I will help," Fuzz said.

He picked up a long stick.

Chapter 4

"What are you doing with that stick?" Cork asked.

"I will scratch the itch for you," Fuzz said.

"You will poke me in the eye!" Cork said.

"I will be careful," Fuzz said.

The stick did not poke Cork in the eye.

It poked Cork in the belly.

"Ouch!" Cork yelled.

Then he fell on Fuzz.

"Ooof!"

The seed puff blew out of Cork's nose.

"Ooof!"

The air blew out of Fuzz's belly.

"I am sorry I fell on you," Cork said.

"I am sorry you have not gotten taller," Fuzz said.

"Or lighter."

Cork helped Fuzz to his feet.
Then he shook Fuzz's paw.
"It was nice being best friends,"
Cork said.
"But we *are* best friends!" Fuzz said.
"No," said Cork.
"We are too different.
I am older than you.
You are taller than me.
There is no way to change that.
Good-bye, Fuzz."
Cork walked toward his home
in the pond.
Fuzz looked after him.
He sniffed.
"Good-bye, Cork," he whispered.

A tear slipped out of his eye
and landed on a nut.
Fuzz picked up the nut.
Then he picked up another nut.
He jumped up
and ran after Cork.
“Cork!” he yelled. “Wait!”
When Fuzz reached Cork,
he held out the two nuts.

"See these nuts?" Fuzz said.

"Are they the same?"

"No," Cork said.

"One is big and wet.

One is little and dry."

"They are different," Fuzz said.

"But they are still nuts."

Then Fuzz pulled Cork
to the edge of the pond.
They looked at themselves
in the water.
"See these friends?" Fuzz asked.
"Are they the same?"
"No," Cork said.
"One is short.
One is tall."
"They are different," Fuzz said.

"But they are still friends."

"Just like two nuts?" Cork asked.

"One little and one big?"

"Just like two nuts," Fuzz said.
"Two best friends—
short and tall together."